T0132358

THANK YOU !!

Balboa Press books may be ordered through booksellers or by contacting:

Balboa Press
A Division of Hay House
1663 Liberty Drive
Bloomington, IN 47403
www.balboapress.com
844-682-1282

ISBN: 978-1-9822-6659-2 (sc)
ISBN: 978-1-9822-6660-8 (e)

Library of Congress Control Number: 2021906907

Print information available on the last page.

Balboa Press rev. date: 06/03/2021

A DIVISION OF HAY HOUSE

Thank The Voice In Your Head

I dedicate this book to my grand-daughter, Ayla,
whose imagination and creativity continue to inspire me.

One day I noticed someone from inside my head was talking to me.

When did this person get into my head? How did he/she/it get there? Who is that?

And why is it telling me things that are making me feel scared? Is there another person living in my head?

Or am I imagining things?

I decided to listen more carefully and I noticed it was trying to keep me away from danger, as if everything and everyone were dangerous.

I left the house to go visit my friend in my neighborhood, and as I wanted to cross the street, the voice in my head said out loud "NO! DON'T DO THAT! YOU WILL GET HIT BY A CAR!"

So I turned around and came back home.

I decided to make myself some tea so I can study for my exam the next day. I went into the kitchen to put the kettle on the stove, when I heard it say to me:

"Stop! DON'T DO THAT! YOU'LL BURN YOURSELF!"

4

So I came to my study room very disappointed and started studying for my test when I heard the voice say:

"STOP WASTING YOUR TIME, YOU WILL NEVER AMOUNT TO ANYTHING!" "YOU ARE SO STUPID!"

"YOU ARE NO GOOD!"

Ugh! What was happening to me? Was I going crazy?

I went in front of the mirror to look and see if I could see this person, this voice who had decided to occupy my head! But instead I heard it say "YOU ARE SO FAT!" "YOU ARE SO UGLY!" "NO ONE LOVES YOU!"

But I didn't see anyone other than myself in the mirror!!!

I found myself so frozen with fear with everything I wanted to do, that I decided to crawl into my bed and pulled the blanket over my head.I just wanted to go to sleep so I wouldn't hear that voice anymore.

When I woke up, I didn't hear anything for a few minutes but it all started again.

Now I was really angry. I felt like I had no control over my life, I felt like I wanted to punch this person/ this voice in my head and tell it to stop talking to me. Yes there were things I had to be careful about. But why should I listen to it? I was already listening to my parents, was that not enough?

And yet I found myself listening more and more as if it was the boss of me!

I went to my younger sister and told her about the person in my head. She started giggling and laughing, and shrugged her shoulders.

She didn't know what I was talking about. I quickly realized that this voice only talks with older kids and grown ups.

Then I went to my mom and asked her if she had a voice in her head talking to her.

She smiled and to my surprise she said "yes", and we call that voice "MIND". Everyone has it. Some people are able to control their mind better than others. Some people become friends with their mind and some people challenge their mind by playing games with it!

I thanked my mom and went about my day.

Next I went to my dad and asked him the same question:

"Is there someone talking to you from your head too?"

My dad smiled and said: "Yes, you mean my mind?"

"It is something all human beings have and not everyone learns about it as quickly as you have!"

I thanked my dad and went about my day.

I love games, so I decided to play games with my Mind! And to start to tell this voice, to my MIND, what *I WANTED* it to tell me instead of what *IT* told me.

Every time my mind said something to me, instead of getting angry or feeling sad or scared, I said "Thank you for sharing, Mind, I've got this! I don't need your opinion!" and went about my day with confidence and a big smile on my face.

I love basketball and always dreamt I could play in the team but because I am small, I never thought it possible. I started imagining that I was on my school's basketball team and even though I was short, I imagined myself running fast with the ball in between the players and throwing the ball in the basket from far away. Wow! That felt so good that I kept on imagining throwing the ball in the hoop and the crowd's loud cheer and clapping for me, I couldn't stop smiling, it felt like magic. I couldn't get enough of it!

I decided to imagine all the things I wanted to do when I grew up. It was so good to feel good. No longer did I feel that I was at the mercy of the voice inside my head, now I was able to push it away by thinking and imagining things that I wanted to be, do, and have. This gave me the courage to imagine more, to dream and dream big. My mood changed and I felt very happy, I felt like I could do anything I wanted!

So every day, I kept imagining all the things I wanted to be, do, and have when I grow up, and one day, one very magical day, I was asked to go to the Principal's office. There I saw the basketball coach who greeted me with a smile! He asked "Would you like to play in the team?"

What?!!! Did I hear that right? Me? I get to play in the school basketball team?

I was so excited I started to cry. "Yes, yes, yes" I said screaming with excitement and hugged the coach. This is magic I thought!

I told the voice inside my head: "I love you, VOICE! I love you, MIND! Thank you for always telling me about the things I didn't like, thank you for always warning me about what's wrong and what's bad, and thank you for always making me doubt myself. If it wasn't for your persistence, I would never be able to discover my own SUPER POWERS!

Now I know that anything I want is possible as long as I want it bad enough. All I need to do is: imagine it, and imagine it again and again and again until it makes me believe I can have it.

I have to remember that you are always pointing out what's *wrong* with me, with the world I live in, with the people in it, and with what I want to do, and so when I listen to you, I feel sad, lonely and unloved!

You never tell me what's *right* with anything or anyone, so I have to keep feeding you all the things that make me feel good.

I know you think you are being good to me and want to be my friend and I love you for that but if you want me to listen to you, and I will when what you say makes me feel good, then you have to listen to whatever I tell you!

I know now that if *I COULD* be in my school's basketball team, even though I am small compared to other kids in the team, then anyone reading this book can do whatever they want, too.

So what is it you wish to be or do or have that your mind is telling you that you can't? If you want it bad enough, just know that you CAN! You just have to start imagining...everyday, as many times as you can, because if it is what you really want, then it will bring a smile to your face and make you happy.

What are some of your dreams that you would like to achieve but your mind is stopping you and telling you that you can't?

Make a list of these dreams, however small or big, and just know that if you take time every day to think about those dreams and imagine yourself achieving them, you will notice the smile they bring to your face. Just keep imagining them when you find the time to do it. You may have one or more dreams, so on the next page you can list your dreams and start imagining away....

A list of my dreams:

1.

2.

3.

4.

5.

6.

7.

8.

9.

10.

Printed in the United States
by Baker & Taylor Publisher Services